GRACIE
The Public Gardens Duck

Story by Judith Meyrick

Illustrations by Richard Rudnicki

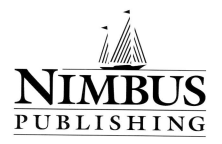

NIMBUS
PUBLISHING

DISCARDED

Copyright text © Judith Meyrick, 2007
Copyright illustrations© Richard Rudnicki, 2007

All rights reserved. No part of this book may be reproduced, stored in a retrieval
system or transmitted in any form or by any means without the prior written
permission from the publisher, or, in the case of photocopying or other reprographic
copying, permission from Access Copyright, 1 Yonge Street, Suite 1900,
Toronto, Ontario M5E 1E5.

Nimbus Publishing Limited
PO Box 9166
Halifax, NS B3K 5M8
(902) 455-4286

Printed and bound in Canada

Design: Heather Bryan
Photo Judith: Stef Reid
Photo Richard: Susan Tooke

Library and Archives Canada Cataloguing in Publication

Meyrick, Judith
Gracie, the Public Gardens duck / Judith Meyrick ;
illustrated by Richard Rudnicki.
Hardcover ISBN 13: 978-1-55109-605-6, ISBN 10: 1-55109-605-6
Softcover ISBN 13: 978-1-55109-645-2, IISBN 10: 1-55109-645-5

1. Ducks—Juvenile fiction. I. Rudnicki, Richard II. Title.

PS8626.E97G73 2007   jC813'.6   C2007-902420-3

We acknowledge the financial support of the Government of Canada through the Book Publishing
Industry Development Program (BPIDP) and the Canada Council, and of the Province of Nova Scotia
through the Department of Tourism, Culture and Heritage for our publishing activities.

Dedication

For Mum—JM

For my mom, who saved
the ducklings—RR

Gracie was hungry. It was early morning in the Halifax Public Gardens and she was ready for breakfast.

Gracie launched herself into the cool water of the fountain, fluffing her feathers as the spray sprinkled around her. She hopped from the water, settled herself in a patch of reeds, and waited patiently.

The gates of the Public Gardens would soon be unlocked, and Mr. Black Suit usually arrived shortly after. He would sit on the park bench to drink his coffee. And he always shared his breakfast with her.

Muffins, thought Gracie as Mr. Black Suit appeared around the bend. *That looks like a muffin bag. Oh, yummy.*

Mr. Black Suit tore open the small white paper bag and began to eat.

"Quack," said Gracie gently, as a little reminder in case Mr. Black Suit had missed her among the reeds. But he kept eating.

"Quack, quack," said Gracie, just a little louder in case Mr. Black Suit had not heard her the first time. But Mr. Black Suit took a sip of his coffee and kept on eating. His muffin got smaller.

"QUACK!" Gracie was worried now. "QUACK, QUACK, QUACK!"

Mr. Black Suit finished the muffin. He stood up and brushed the crumbs off the knees of his carefully pressed black pants.

"Sorry, old friend," he said. And he left the gardens through the swinging gate, crossed the road, and vanished into the CBC building.

Gracie's beak dropped. Something was definitely wrong. Mr. Black Suit always shared his breakfast with her.

Two Sacred Heart girls passed her, munching breakfast bagels as they walked to school on the other side of the park.

"Quack," she called to them.

"Sorry, Mrs. Duck," they called back.

Gracie's stomach rumbled loudly. She sighed and began to waddle toward the concession near the bandstand, where they sold popcorn that people liked to share with the ducks. It wasn't her favourite breakfast and she would have to compete for it with those pushy Public Gardens pigeons. But Gracie was hungry. She'd take what she could get.

A little girl skipped toward her as Gracie trudged along the gravel path past the lake.

"Quack?" she said hopefully.

"What is it?" asked the little girl. She crouched low and peered at Gracie.

"Quack," said Gracie. "Quaaaack."

"Oh," said the little girl. "You're hungry?" She bounced to her feet and called to her mother, who appeared by the bend in the path. "Mom," she said, opening her lunchbox. "I'm just going to give the duck some of my peanut butter sandwich."

Gracie's heart leapt. Peanut butter! She LOVED peanut butter sandwiches. Especially with honey. But then again, peanut butter any old way would be just fine. It was her absolute favourite. Good thing she hadn't filled up on crumbly old muffins from Mr. Black Suit. She fluffed her wings, wobbled her tail a little, and said "Quack" in a very pleased sort of way.

"Alice," said the girl's mother. "That's not such a good idea. Remember the sign at the gates?"

"Oh, right," Alice said. "I forgot." She snapped her lunchbox closed. "Sorry, duck." She slipped her hand into her mother's and the two continued on their way through the park.

"Sign? What sign?" Gracie yelled after them. "And what about that peanut butter sandwich? I'm okay without honey."

But all they heard was a sorrowful QUAAACK!

Gracie was truly worried now. But also puzzled. Park People always fed the ducks. Sometimes she would waddle up beside them and take the offered food right from their hands. That made them laugh and she got the best treats that way. What was wrong? Why was no one giving her breakfast?

Gracie followed Alice and her mother toward the gate.

"Quack," she said again. "Are you sure?"

Alice looked back and waved. "Sorry, duck," she called again. "Look!" She pointed.

"AAAK!" squawked Gracie. While there were a lot of words Gracie couldn't read, the bold letters along the bottom were clear enough...PLEASE DO NOT FEED THE DUCKS.

IMPORTANT NOTICE

The majority of the ducks in park areas are wild, and feeding them may result in their failure to migrate. This will have a major impact on their health, natural habits and on the sustainability of park environments.

PLEASE DO NOT FEED THE DUCKS

This was terrible. Belly rumbling, she waddled back toward the fountain and tucked herself under an azalea bush to think. She thought hard for a long time. And at the end of her thinking, she had A PLAN. She would need some paint, any colour would do. And she knew just where to find it. She wandered nonchalantly over to the Rose Garden, where early roses were just beginning to bloom. A lone artist was setting up his easel. Gracie sidled over.

"Quack," said Gracie as she watched the artist settle himself on a tiny folding stool and begin to work.

"Hello, duck," said the artist as he opened a tube of yellow paint, squeezed a big blob on his palette, and dropped it back into the paint box without replacing the lid.

Gracie waited a moment, then leaned in and plucked the tube from the box. Holding it firmly in her mouth, she waddled quickly back to the azalea bush, where she carefully hid the paint in the undergrowth. Then she settled into a cozy hollow, tucked her head under her wing, and napped the afternoon away.

That night, after the gates were closed and padlocked, Gracie put her plan into action. Taking the tube of yellow paint, she smeared some on the bottom of her webbed foot and flew to the gate. Her plan was simple. She would need to hover like a hummingbird drinking nectar from a tall flower. But she soon found out that hovering is very awkward for a duck. In fact, it turned out that hovering is an ENORMOUS CHALLENGE if you're not a hummingbird!

But she didn't give up. She was too hungry. She kept on hovering and flapping and huffing until finally, she did it. With a triumphant "QUACK," she managed to plant her painted foot firmly on the sign in exactly the right place. Then she washed the leftover yellow paint off her foot and went to bed feeling hugely pleased with herself. People coming through the swinging gate the next day would now see this:

PLEASE DO FEED THE DUCKS

The next morning, Gracie waited patiently for Mr. Black Suit. He arrived right on time but gently shook his head.

"I don't know," he said to Gracie. "The sign doesn't look quite right to me."

Gracie quacked a little desperately. She was very hungry now. And it looked like there was a carrot muffin in the small white paper bag. But all her quacking and prancing did no good whatsoever. Mr. Black Suit ate the whole muffin and Gracie remained hungry.

For the rest of the morning, Gracie wandered the Public Gardens looking for food, getting hungrier and hungrier. She quacked at children eating ice cream. She quacked at people hurrying to their offices. She quacked loudly for help when she got stuck upside down in a garbage bin trying to retrieve an apple core. Fortunately, a grounds-keeper came to her rescue. But by lunchtime, Gracie was still hungry and feeling weaker by the minute. She was beginning to think she would never eat again.

Dejectedly, she picked about the grass looking for crumbs. But there were none. Only little insects under the grass. Gracie was so hungry that she ate some before she realized what was happening. To her surprise, she found them quite tasty. Really quite tasty. She ate some more. Yummy!

The sun rose high overhead. Gracie was feeling much better after her surprise snack and she slipped into the lake for a swim, zipping around and around the little white ship moored in the middle. She snuffled her beak in the water to cool off. What was that? She peered in the water. Trailing plant stuff caught on her foot. Gracie pulled it off with her beak. Hmmmm, a bit different, she thought as she nibbled, but good.

She could see plant tendrils waving below the surface. If she held her feet together and gave a kick, sort of backwards and up, then her tail tipped into the air, her head went straight down, and she was able to feed on the tasty morsels below. She kicked and gobbled and quacked and splashed, then kicked and gobbled some more. It was a lot of fun.

Gracie spent the rest of the day playing and swimming. She practised bobbing upside down for snacks and waddled through the grass looking for lunch. Then she swam some more in the fountain and went to sleep feeling contented and quite, quite full. She realized that the Public Gardens had plenty of food for her to eat and that she probably wouldn't starve after all.

The next morning, Gracie was waiting for Mr. Black Suit once again in the reeds along the edge of the fountain near the corner swinging gate. While Mr. Black Suit ate his muffin, Gracie grazed for her breakfast in the grass nearby.

"Well done, old friend," said Mr. Black Suit. "Looks like you've figured this out pretty quickly."

"Quack, Quack," said Gracie, in a pleased sort of way.